leapfrog

The Elves
and the Shoemaker

First published in 2006 by
Franklin Watts
338 Euston Road
London
NW1 3BH

Franklin Watts Australia
Hachette Children's Books
Level 17/207 Kent Street
Sydney
NSW 2000

A CIP catalogue record for this book is available
from the British Library.

ISBN 0 7496 6575 0 (hbk)
ISBN 0 7496 6581 5 (pbk)

Series Editor: Jackie Hamley
Series Advisor: Dr Barrie Wade
Series Designer: Peter Scoulding

Printed in China

The Elves
and the Shoemaker

Retold by Karen Wallace

Illustrated by Andy Catling

FRANKLIN WATTS
LONDON•SYDNEY

Once there lived a
poor shoemaker.

He was so poor that
he could only buy leather
for one pair of shoes.

"I will make the shoes in the morning," he said sadly to his wife. Then they went to bed.

7

Next morning,
the shoemaker
was amazed!

The leather had been made into a pair of beautiful shoes!

That day, he sold the
shoes and bought
more leather with
the money.

Next morning, the shoemaker was astounded. There were two pairs of beautiful shoes on his table!

They were so lovely that
the shoemaker sold them
straight away.

Months passed.

Each day, the shoemaker
bought more leather.

And next morning, he
found new shoes. Soon
the shoemaker was rich.

"We must find out who is helping us," said the shoemaker's wife.
So, one night, they hid and waited.

At midnight, two elves jumped in through the window.

They had ragged jackets and bare feet.

Quick as a flash, they made the leather into shoes.

Then they disappeared.

"I will make the elves some warm clothes to say thank you," said the wife.

"And I will make them shoes," said the shoemaker.

They left the clothes and
shoes on the table and
waited until midnight.

When the elves saw the clothes and shoes, they quickly put them on.

Then they danced for joy
and skipped out of the
window.

The elves never came
back, but the shoemaker
and his wife ...

... lived happily ever after.

Leapfrog has been specially designed to fit the requirements of the National Literacy Strategy. It offers real books for beginning readers by top authors and illustrators.
There are 49 Leapfrog stories to choose from: